Rescue Tails

THE TREACHEROUS TOWER

Also from StacyPlays

Rescue Tails

THE TREACHEROUS TOWER

Stacy Plays

ILLUSTRATED BY Mélody Gringoire

HARPER
An Imprint of HarperCollinsPublishers

Library of Congress Control Number: 2023931278
ISBN 978-0-06-322499-5
Typography by Catherine Lee
23 24 25 26 27 LBC 6 5 4 3 2

First Edition

Rescue Tails

THE TREACHEROUS TOWER

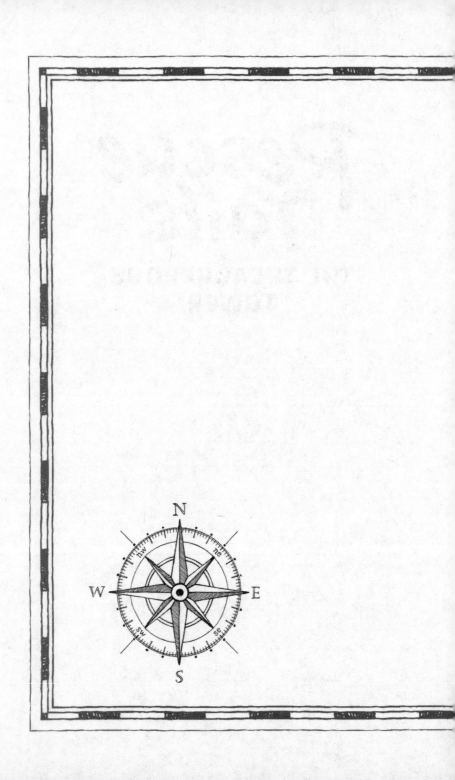

FRIDAY

DAY 1

4:39 p.m.

I thought today was going to be an uneventful day. Wrong! Something big is about to happen. REALLY BIG. It started out as a pretty normal day in my life. I woke up and then went to the kitchen to feed my cats, Milquetoast and Pipsqueak.

As soon as my cats were finished eating, they both curled up in front of the fireplace and went back to sleep. Must be nice, I thought. As for me, I had to get ready for school. I got dressed, packed my bag, and quickly ate my breakfast. I had a bowl of porridge with some eggs (from my chicken, Fluff) and berries.

As I was leaving for school, I played a quick game of fetch with my dogs, Page and Molly. Well . . . I guess I really just played fetch with Page. Molly refuses to hold a dirty stick in her mouth. She just

watches while Page and I play with the stick.

At school, the first subject of the day

was math. I aced the pop quiz except for one

question that really had my head spinning! If I'm being honest, I don't like math. English and art are my favorite subjects. I guess that's why I mostly write and draw in this journal instead of solving math equations—ha!

$$(-2)(-1)(-3)(-4)(-1) = -24!!!!!!!!$$

I'll get it right next time. Sorry, Addi!

At lunch, Mathilda Lemming teased me because of my outfit. Like I said, today started out like any other day in my life. That's because Mathilda Lemming makes fun of what I wear EVERY SINGLE DAY. She always manages to find something she doesn't like about my clothes. Sometimes it's the color of my pants or the pattern of my shirt. Last week, she didn't like that I wore the same outfit on Thursday that I'd worn on Monday. I swear she must be keeping her own journal of what I wear! Today, she made fun of my overalls and the fact that there was mud down the back of them. I try not to let what she says get to me, but a couple of my other classmates laughed along with her.

When lunch was over, I ran to the bathroom and tried to wash the mud off before going

back to class. I guess I won't be wearing overalls to school anymore. . . . I don't know how to make Mathilda stop teasing me. Maybe she would stop if I could think of a really good comeback to say to her. I could have said that for someone with the word *math* in her name, she really isn't the best at algebra. But that would be mean, and I don't want to be mean.

More than anything, what I really wanted to do was tell her how the mud got there. I wanted to say it's because I spent yesterday

Mathilda? More like MEANilda

afternoon hanging out with my pack of wolves in the forest where I live!!

Everest   Basil   Addison   Noah   Tucker   Wink

Then she would have understood that I only got mud on my clothes because I was out foraging for mushrooms for dinner. My wolf Addison is a really good cook and can tell which mushrooms are safe to eat and which ones are poisonous. I bet Mathilda can't do that!

The truth is I get mud and dirt on my clothes all the time. It happens pretty much whenever I'm doing things with my wolf pack. We're always off exploring the taiga (that's the name of the type of forest we live in) and tending to our vegetable garden. And we're constantly collecting sticks and chopping wood to use in our fireplace. Or tidying up our cave since it can get pretty messy with six wolves, two dogs, two cats, a chicken, and a human.

chanterelle mushroom

morel mushroom

fairy ring mushroom

And then sometimes I get mud on my overalls doing the VERY most important thing my wolves and I do . . . **rescuing animals**! We're always running around the forest helping animals who are trapped or hurt.

I can't tell Mathilda the truth, though. I can't tell anyone. I keep my wolf pack a secret from everyone at school. There's no way in a MILLION years anyone would believe the truth. Sometimes I wonder what would actually happen if I raised my hand and announced to the class that both of my parents are dead and that I live in the woods with a pack of wolves who can understand every word I say, including one named Addison who taught me how to do math and makes breakfast for me every morning—AND we go on secret trips all over the world to help save animals in trouble!

Yeah . . . I can't imagine that going very well. I'm also afraid of what would happen if they did believe me. People think wolves are dangerous. Most humans don't know how to live peacefully alongside the apex predators that live in the forest like wolves, bears, and mountain lions.

Apex predators are animals at the top of the food chain!

I wish I could show people those animals want to be left alone to hunt their food and take care of their young. I guess I'm just lucky that I get to have six wolves in my family.

Yep, Mathilda would never believe what a cool life I have in the forest, even if she saw me riding Everest to school. Sometimes I wish I could show her, just to see the look on her face.

ANYWAY . . . enough about Mathilda Lemming and back to what made today so eventful. When I got home from school, Milo the bat was fluttering around the cave. I could tell from the urgent way he was flapping his wings that he'd heard an animal was in trouble. Like I said, I've started rescuing animals in my spare time with the help of my pack. We used to only help animals that we discovered were in trouble near our cave. But when I rescued Page and realized that she could understand Milo, we began getting calls for help from all over the forest. And then from around the world!

Since then, we've gone on rescue missions to the mesa, the tundra, and even the deep ocean. We've rescued donkeys, narwhals, dolphins, and even an entire coral reef!

Oh, I forgot to mention how we can

understand Milo's missions. Some bats, like

Milo, use echolocation, which means they send

out pulses of

noise that bounce

off things around

them. Normally

they use that to

learn about their

surroundings,

but Milo's sound

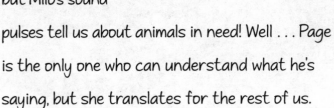

pulses tell us about animals in need! Well . . . Page

is the only one who can understand what he's

saying, but she translates for the rest of us.

Anyway, Milo flew over to where Page was

standing. Page's ears swiveled, and then she

trotted over to the globe on my desk. Page spun

the globe with her nose and rested it on a patch of land.

Just as I suspected, there *is* an animal that needs our help urgently. And that animal lives in . . . **THE JUNGLE!**

I've read a little about jungles in books I've checked out from the library, but I've never been to one in real life. There are so many animals in the jungle that I've never seen before. In fact, there are more unique animal species in jungle rain forests than anywhere else in the entire world. But looking for

just one animal there would be like looking for a needle in a haystack. I had to narrow down what type of animal needed our help. So I asked Page a series of questions:

Is the animal old?

Is it young? *WOOF!*

Does it fly?

Does it swim?

Does it walk? *WOOF!*

Does it have fur?

WOOF!

Stripes?

What about spots?

WOOF! WOOF!!

Okay, so it's a young animal that walks on land and has spotted fur. I thought about it for a minute. Then I looked at Page and said, "Is the animal a baby ocelot?" Page started zooming around the cave excitedly. We had our mission!

I've got to get to the jungle as fast as I can. But there's a lot to do before I leave. I've been

frantically packing everything I can think of. I
hope I don't forget something.

The
hardest part
of going on
these rescue
missions isn't
packing. It's
deciding which
wolf should
come with me.
Every wolf

- ☑ Raincoat!!
- ☑ Binoculars
- ☑ Lantern
- ☑ Pickaxe
- ☑ Canteen
- ☑ Compass
- ☑ Waterproof bag
- ☑ Watch
- ☐ Rescue journal
- ☐ Snacks?
- ☐ Piranha repellant!?!

in my pack has a supernatural ability. Noah is
an amazing swimmer. Basil is reeaaallly fast.
Addison has super intelligence (she's so good at
solving puzzles). Everest is the strongest and
can read my mind. Tucker is a healer. And Wink

is indestructible. I don't have time to recount the whole story of how they got those abilities, but let's just say that their talents have come in very handy over the years. And they have even saved my life on more than one occasion!

I really wish I could bring all the wolves with me to the jungle. But walking around with an entire wolf pack following me is pretty **conspicuous**. (Do you like that word? It was on my vocabulary quiz this week and it means something stands out in an obvious way.) And since my life with my wolf pack is **TOP SECRET**, it's best to only bring one of them with me. Besides, it's not like the wolves who stay behind don't have plenty to do. They have to take care of the dogs and cats and keep watch for trouble in the taiga.

The wolves who don't come will miss me while

I'm gone. (What's not to miss? Ha ha!) But I'm usually only away for a couple of days. And this time I might be back even sooner because the wolf I have selected to come with me is . . . **Basil**.

Yep, Basil is the fastest wolf in my pack. Ever since she got struck by lightning, that is! That's a looooong story and I don't exactly have time to write it right now, but I'll just say this . . . any time I oversleep for school, I ask Basil to give me a ride so I won't be late!

I'm going to bring Basil to the jungle with me

because it's a long journey. The jungle is several days away, and we need to get there as fast as we can. We also have to come home quickly so I don't miss any school.

Basil was *thrilled* when I told her the news. In fact, she's already dashing around the cave gathering all the supplies we need. She just brought me a bundle of dry tinder she collected outside. Basil is so smart! The rain forest will be very wet. We'll use these twigs and pine needles to make our campfires there. I put it all in a plastic bag to keep it dry and then stuffed the bag into my satchel. I'd better go and help her finish packing. We're going to leave the second we're done. We'll run through the night. But first we need to make one special stop. . . .

6:01 p.m.

Whew! I made it to the library right as it was closing. I had just enough time to run in and find the books I'll need about the jungle. Thank goodness nobody else had checked them out already.

I love the library so much! I check books
out for myself and Addison (she can't exactly
get her own library card) all the time. I've even
made friends with the librarian. When I walked
to the front desk with an armful of books about
the jungle, she asked me if I was doing a school
report. I told a little white lie. I said I was just
curious and wanted to read more. I couldn't
exactly tell her that I was actually leaving to go
to the jungle on a rescue mission!

I'm going to take two of the books I got with me on the trip. One is about all the different kinds of mammals that live in the jungle. The other one is about the birds, reptiles, fish, and amphibians I may encounter there. Oh, I forgot to say the best part . . . they're both paperbacks! They won't be too heavy in my bag. I'm going to go find where Basil is hiding, and then we're heading back into the cover of the forest to start traveling south. Who knows where I'll be the next time I can write again.

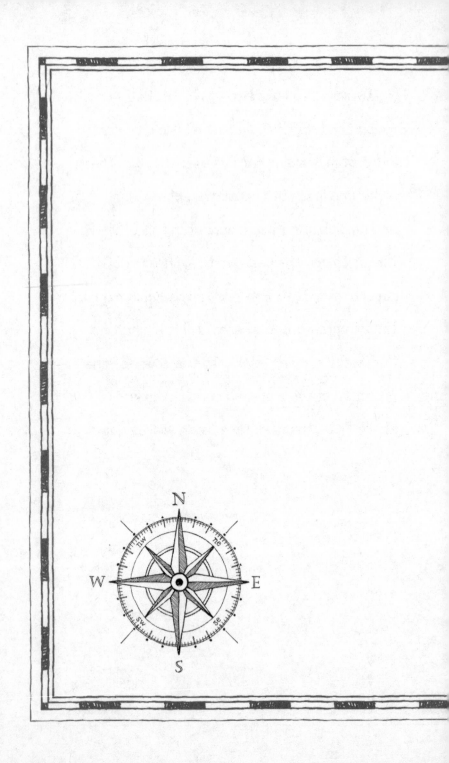

SATURDAY

DAY 2

6:12 a.m.

Basil outdid herself!! I just woke up after a VERY bumpy night of riding on her back . . . only to discover that she made it even farther than I'd hoped! We're already farther south than I've ever been before. Basil stopped to rest at the most BEAUTIFUL lake I've ever seen. And that's saying a lot, because there are some really pretty lakes near our cave. As soon as she stopped running, Basil waded into the water and drank a lot. She must have been so thirsty! Now she's fast asleep. Luckily there's no one around, so it should be safe to rest here. Basil probably won't wake up for a few hours. I know we don't have time to lose on our way to this rescue mission, but she clearly needs the sleep.

It's taking a lot of concentration right now

to update my rescue journal instead of looking around at the scenery in this new biome. There are tall trees surrounding the entire lake, with water lilies floating at the edges. I think I'll walk around the perimeter of the lake and explore a bit while Basil recharges.

9:23 a.m.

You will never believe what I found! While I was standing at the edge of the water, a small green fish swam up to me. I took off my boots and socks and rolled up my pants and waded into the water and that's when I realized . . . it wasn't a fish at all. It was an **axolotl**!!! It's a really rare amphibian with external gills. Usually, when you see a fish's gills, they're those little slits on the sides of their bodies, but axolotls have something called gill rakers. Gill rakers are their own personal water filters that look like a silly hairdo on their head. I never thought in a BILLION years I'd ever get to see an axolotl in the wild. It swam around my ankles for a little while, and I managed to sketch it.

Such a happy little creature! Finding an axolotl here means that this lake is filled with **brackish water**. Brackish water is saltier 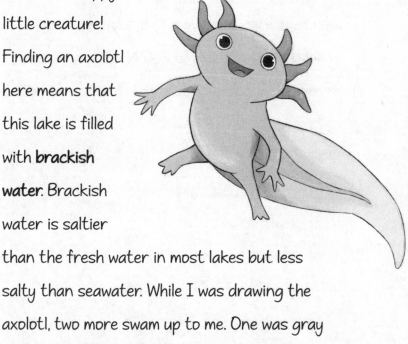 than the fresh water in most lakes but less salty than seawater. While I was drawing the axolotl, two more swam up to me. One was gray and the other one was brown. I remember

reading in a book that axolotls are incredibly
endangered animals, partly because people have
introduced non-native fish (fish that normally
spawn somewhere else in the world) to the lakes
the axolotls live in. Sometimes these non-native
fish eat the axolotls' young! I can't understand
why people would move a fish from one body
of water to another. My wolf Noah is quite the
expert at catching fish. If only Noah were here,

I'd tell him to catch as many non-native fish as he could! It's not that I want him to kill all the non-native fish. It just that they're not supposed to be here. It's not their fault people brought them here, but it's also not right that axolotls might go **EXTINCT** because humans have been so careless. Even just thinking about that makes me so sad.

Maybe we can come back and do something to protect the axolotls' habitat. I could honestly stay here all day watching them swim, but I can see Basil stirring on the other side of the lake. It won't be long before she's ready to run again. I'll try to write another update soon.

1:14 p.m.

We finally reached the giant region of flooded grasslands called the Pantanal! Basil was running along as usual, and then, all of a sudden, I heard splashing. The next thing I knew . . . we were both soaked! Basil has to tread carefully because her legs are completely underwater. But now that she's slowly wading through the water, she's steady enough that I just couldn't wait to pull my rescue journal from my bag and log an update.

The jungle can't be far now. Even if the water gets deeper, Basil is a pretty good swimmer. Not as good as Noah, but who is? Maybe we can make it to the jungle before nightfall. I just pulled out my compass and we're heading east now. We just passed a pink **ipê**—a gorgeous tree with pink flowers—and I just can't believe . . .

1:21 p.m.

Sorry I stopped writing there. I saw something BIG in the water! Turns out, it was a GIANT RIVER OTTER. It swam up right next to Basil and me.

Cute, right? But also, a little intimidating! I'm used to seeing otters back home, but this species of otter is double

the size of a normal river otter. The otter was **periscoping**—a swimming move where they show off the unique markings on their neck and try to appear bigger to a potential threat. The giant river otter seemed to be checking us out. I'm guessing they've never seen someone riding on a wolf in the water before. They tend to live in groups. A group of giant river otters is called a **holt**. Giant river otters are really impressive hunters. They feast on fish (even piranhas!), frogs, snakes, and sometimes small caiman (a reptile that is related to the alligator). They also defend their territory if they feel threatened. And sure enough, as soon as the giant otter got close to us, he started making a really high-pitched noise, almost like a scream.

"Go, Basil!" I shouted. Basil sped off. As we waded around a cluster of trees, I saw the rest of the holt playing on the shore of the wetlands.

That was probably the most danger we've been in so far. Which is to say that it's been pretty smooth sailing on this rescue mission.

5:29 p.m.

Speaking of smooth sailing . . . guess what Basil
and I found? A boat!!! Right by the giant river
otters, the wetlands gave way to a large river.
Just as Basil was getting ready to dive in, I
spotted an old wooden rowboat. The tiny boat
looked abandoned,
but it was the
perfect size for us.
It didn't spring any
leaks and I used
the oars to paddle

The boat we found!

43

us down the river so Basil could get a little rest.

Traveling through the Pantanal wetlands with Basil has been the most magical experience. Sure, it was . . . damp. My fingers and toes still look like shriveled-up prunes even though we've been out of the water for a while. There were a few times where the river was smooth, and I could stop paddling and draw while the current took us deeper into the wilderness. I saw a caiman sleeping on a rock, a group of marsh deer, and a great kiskadee—an amazingly colorful bird with

a yellow body, brown wings, and a black-and-white head that looked a little like a badger.

So many incredible wild animals! I even spotted a ring-tailed coati in a meadow. It looked just like my cat Pip. I've drawn both of them for reference. I think it's the tail. . . .

Speaking of wild animals . . . my hair does not like the humidity in this biome. I caught a glimpse of my reflection in the water and couldn't believe how frizzy my hair was. Good thing Mathilda Lemming can't see me right now.

Back to the rescue mission: I'm pretty sure that a small ocelot would be in a dense jungle, not a meadow or a marsh. So, we have left the boat and the Pantanal and are heading into the forest now. Our pace has slowed considerably because there's not a lot of open space for Basil to run. There are branches and vines everywhere.

Oh, you know how I was worried I would forget to pack something back at the cave when we left in such a hurry? Well, it finally dawned on me what it was that I forgot. My knife! It would have really come in handy right now. I could help Basil cut back some of the tangled obstacles blocking our path. That said, we are also trying to tread lightly. We don't want to disturb the ecosystem any more than we have to. But once in a while, we have no choice but to clear the way. And because I don't have a knife, Basil is mostly doing it with her teeth. She's gnawing her way through a particularly dense patch of vines right now, which has given me a chance to write this entry.

It's always dark here in the trees, but I think it's actually getting dark outside the forest

My knife back at home in the cave. Grrr!

now. Night is coming, so we need to keep our eyes out for a place to set up camp. It's been such a long day. I can't wait to be warm and cozy by the fire that Basil will make. My boots and socks are still soaked from the wetlands, so it will be good to get them dried. Maybe we'll even make something warm to eat.

9:39 p.m.

I will try my best to write this entry, but my fingers are still cold and wet. The pen keeps slipping out of my hand. I didn't get that warm fire I was dreaming of. I wrote my last entry as we were entering this forest. Well, it turns out, it's a RAIN FOREST. It started raining a couple of hours ago, and it does not look like it'll be letting up anytime soon. Thank goodness I remembered my jacket. Basil and I crafted a tent out of some enormous fronds we collected from the rain forest floor. As long as I curl up next to her, I'll be warm. I can't wait to show my drawing of our tent to the other wolves back home. I think it will remind them a little bit of a shelter we made once on a tropical island.

In school, I learned that rain forests can get more than three hundred inches of rain in a year. That's so much rain! It might make it uncomfortable for Basil and me, but it's why everything here is so lush and green. If I lived here, I would be covered in mud all the time. . . . I'd never hear the end of it from Mathilda Lemming. Yep, even though I'm hundreds of miles away from school, I'm still thinking about that. It's not like I haven't considered buying some new outfits, but I can't afford to get new clothes. Even if I could, I wouldn't have anywhere to keep them. I don't exactly have a walk-in closet in my cave. Part of me wishes that my school made us wear uniforms. Maybe then Mathilda would leave me alone. Who am I kidding? She'd probably start teasing me about other things like my hair or the shape of my nose—things I couldn't change even if I wanted to.

I love my hair! And my nose!

I really don't know what to do about Mathilda, but I guess that's a problem for when I get home. Right now, I need to find the baby ocelot Milo sent us here to rescue.

I'm going to read a little more of my books and then try to get some sleep. In the morning, I want to climb the tallest tree I can find and use my binoculars to decide which direction we should go.

9:48 p.m.

Just kidding, I'm back. A tiny frog wandered into our tent right as I was finishing that last entry!

This has got to be the cutest little frog I've ever seen. According to my book, she's a poison dart frog. The name

sounds a lot scarier than it really is. Its actual name is Dendrobatidae and this one is called an Okopipi. She's my favorite color . . . blue! But frogs like her can come in all kinds of different bright colors like red, yellow, green, and orange. They can have stripes, polka dots—even a combination of patterns!

I'm pretty sure this frog is a female, but I won't know for sure until I get home and check out a library book entirely about frogs. Oh . . . to be clear, I'm not planning on bringing this frog home. That would be very bad. It is best she stays here in the habitat she's used to. After all, her species would have adapted over thousands of years to be best suited for this exact biome. I'm not even going to pick her up, even though I really want to. She can ooze toxins onto my hand that could harm me.

Oh wow, I just read that Patter is

aposematic. Oh, I named her Patter—after

the pitter-patter of rain on our tent. I think

it suits her. **Aposematic** means that the frog's

bright color and patterns protect it by warning

other animals that it would be dangerous to

attack or eat. I think it would be smarter to

blend into the forest like owls or chameleons do, but apparently this strategy works, too! We'll see if Patter is still lurking around our camp in the morning. All right—NOW I am really going to try to get some sleep.

SUNDAY

DAY 3

6:43 a.m.

Wow! The view from up here is absolutely breathtaking. I'm not sure any words could do justice to what I see. If I had to try, here are some of the words I would use: Majestic. Colorful. Inspiring. Noisy. . . . Perfect.

It finally stopped raining early this morning, and Basil helped me to dry out all of my clothes. Patter was nowhere to be found, but that's okay. She probably left to find something to eat while I was sleeping. As soon as the tiny beams of sunlight started to shoot their way in through the leaves of our tent, I set out to find a good tree to climb. I needed one with lots of branches, but I also wanted it to be taller than the trees around it so I could get a good view. And wow, did I ever find the perfect tree. The tree was a kapok tree, I

It's me!

think. It had HUGE roots.

I scrambled up the roots into its branches, and then I shimmied my way up at least 150 feet farther. I'm glad that my wolf Everest can only read my mind when I'm near him. If he knew how high up I was right now, he would be worried sick about me.

Being on top of the canopy of jungle trees is like being in a whole new biome! I've seen at least six different species of birds since I've been up here . . . at least, six that I've been able to identify.

Hoatzin

Toucan

A little strange-looking, but I'm sure they think the same about me!

My absolute favorite bird here has got to be the southern mealy parrot. It's named for the white tinge on its back. It looks as if it's been dusted with flour. One of them even landed on my shoulder while I was drawing. I admired its beautiful green feathers and the cheery yellow patch on top of its head. The book says the population of mealy parrots is decreasing because people are trapping them to sell as pets. I can't imagine keeping a bird like this inside. It should be allowed to fly freely here in the rain forest.

It seems to me that people should only rescue animals like dogs and cats as their pets, since humans are the reason there are so many of them in the world. Creatures that live in the wild like axolotls, frogs, snakes, and birds shouldn't be captured and kept. I wonder what my pets are doing right now. What if they think I've left them forever? That would break my heart. I hope they know I'm going to come home as soon as I can. And that I miss them.

Oh! I forgot! Halfway up the tree, I ran directly into a sloth. Well, we certainly didn't run into each other. We were both

Dragon fruit...my breakfast for today!

climbing the tree . . . me much faster than it. I
can finally confirm from personal experience
that sloths are *ssss-llll-oooo-wwww*. The sloth
had the right of way though, so I waited for
it to cross the branch. I was happy to take a
break from climbing, and it gave me a chance to
get a good look at the sloth as it slowly moved
across the vines.

Its arms were just as long as its legs,
and it had really long, curved claws. The

cream-and-black markings on its face reminded me of the raccoons I see back home. Its body was mostly brown, but the fur on its back had a greenish tint. I pulled the book on mammals out of my bag and looked up the entry about sloths. Apparently, sloths are **arboreal**, which means that they actually live in these trees! Once a week, they climb down to the ground to poop! Once a week? This surprised me, but it actually makes sense because a single leaf can take an entire month to travel through the sloth's four-chambered stomach. I guess everything a sloth does is slow!

Let me in!
I haven't pooped
in a week!

SLOTH
OUTHOUSE

OH WOW! I also just read that the green on its back is algae!!! The sloth moves so slowly, algae actually has time to grow on its fur. This gives the sloth a natural camouflage from predators. The algae also attracts moths who mate on the sloth's back and then lay eggs in its poop! That's so cool! And kind of gross.

Okay, so back to the view from the top of the tree canopy. Thank goodness I brought my binoculars. I can see the Pantanal back the direction we came from. Ahead of me, to the right, is a strange, treeless area with some smoke.  And to the left, there looks to be some type of tower hidden in the trees. Ancient ruins, maybe?

I don't like the look of the clearing with the smoke. It certainly seems like somewhere that a baby ocelot could get into trouble. So that's where we are going to go. It's time to climb down this tree and get on with this rescue. If only I had wings and could fly down instead. . . .

12:05 p.m.

Arghhhh! I am so angry right now. It took so long to climb down the tree—over an hour! And right when I was almost at the bottom, I scraped my arm pretty badly. It hurts a lot, and I didn't bring any bandages with me. I had to tear the sleeve off my shirt to wrap around my arm. I washed it with water the best I could. I hope it doesn't get infected. I just know my wolf Tucker would be able to forage a leaf or something in the rain forest with natural healing properties, but Basil and I are clueless when it comes to the plants around us.

Can't wait to hear what Mathilda thinks of my new look, ha ha!

If that wasn't bad enough, we made it to the clearing and there are people destroying the rain forest! There were huge tractors with pincer-like arms uprooting trees. There were massive trucks with logs bundled on them and bulldozers flattening the ground. The rain forest edge surrounding the cleared area was filled with monkeys, birds, and all kinds of insects. They were lucky to escape the path of the machines, but now they watched helplessly as their habitat was destroyed.

At first, I was sad. I even started to cry. But the more I thought about what was happening, the angrier I got. And then I had an idea. Basil and I waited in the bushes until the people operating the machines left to eat their lunches. One by one, Basil darted around the site, stealing the keys to all the machines. It won't solve the problem, but at least it will slow them down a bit. Hopefully it'll give the animals that live here enough time to look for a new home.

In a way, all the animals that just lost their homes need rescuing. But I haven't seen an ocelot yet. And I

don't think Milo would have sent only Basil and
me down here to solve a problem this big all on
our own. Sure, I've tackled big challenges before,
back in the taiga, but then I had help from
all my wolves and even some humans. There is
still a baby ocelot
out there that
desperately needs
our help. We just
haven't found it
yet. I hate to write
this, but I am
beginning to worry

that we might be too late. It's taken us so long
to get down here to the jungle. And now I have
no idea where to go, and I feel like I really failed
at this rescue mission. That's never happened

before. I can't imagine getting back to the cave
and having to tell all the other wolves that we
couldn't save the little ocelot.

I'm so sorry.
I tried my best.

To make matters worse, we don't have a lot
of food. There's a bit of dried fish left in my bag,
but that's for Basil. We left the awful clearing
site and came back into the jungle in hopes of
finding something to eat. I found some cacao

pods growing on a
tree trunk. . . .

    I was so excited
because chocolate
comes from cacao
pods! I managed to
crack one open on a rock, but it was filled with
hard beans covered in slimy white gunk.

                My book
                said that the
                monkeys that
                live here love
            eating this white
        pulp, so I tasted it—and it's
terrible! Maybe monkeys don't think so, but I
do. Apparently, to make chocolate, I would have
to ferment the beans and then dry them out

and grind them up. I don't have time for that.

So, to recap . . . here I am, with a scraped arm,
a handful of keys, NO CHOCOLATE, and a failed
rescue mission.

I'm not sure things could get any worse.

3:21 p.m.

It got worse.

   Just as I was finishing up that last journal entry, a bat *pooped* right where I was writing! YUCK. Bat poop is called **guano**. My bat, Milo, would never drop any guano in our cave, let alone inside a book of mine! I raised my hand up to shoo the bat away, but I quickly changed my mind as soon as I got a good look at it. The bat was so cute! According to my mammal book, it's a fishing bat, otherwise known as a **bulldog bat** because of its wide snout.

Leave it
to me to find
a bat that's
actually named
after a dog,
right? But
then a thought
occurred to me.
Maybe I didn't

Woof,
woof!

find this bat at all . . . What if this bat found
me? According to the book, this bat species is
an expert at catching fish. They make their
homes in hollow trees and normally live near
a body of water. But we weren't by any water.
Bulldog bats are also nocturnal, and it was
daytime. What if this was the bat who sent the

original rescue message to Milo?

The bat started flying around Basil, nudging her in a particular direction. Yes! This bat must know where we need to go. I got a rush of energy as if I'd eaten ten chocolate bars. We were finally going to find the ocelot we'd come to the jungle to rescue!

I hopped on Basil's back, and we started chasing the bat through the jungle. We ran for several miles until, finally, the bat stopped flying and hovered in one spot. I looked around—my heart sank when I realized where we were. The tower. I saw this place when I was on top of the trees. I chose to investigate the smoke in the clearing instead, wasting precious time. Time that the ocelot might not have. Still, I held out hope. After all, the bulldog bat

wouldn't have brought us here if there wasn't
still a chance that we could save the ocelot.

Basil and I waved goodbye to the bat. It
quickly flew away, probably back to bed where
it belongs at this time of day. I looked up at the
tower. The part of the ruins I'd spotted from
the treetops was a tall tower three or four
stories high.

All of a sudden, something small and spotted darted in front of me. I stumbled back a few steps. Basil crouched near me and started growling a low growl.

"What was that?" I said. "Who's there?"

I turned around in a circle, catching glimpses of spots moving quickly around me. As I jerked my head back and forth trying to figure out what it was, more and more spots appeared until my eyes finally focused on what it was. An ocelot!

The cat was about three feet long and probably weighed over twenty-five pounds. She was much bigger than Pipsqueak—and that's saying something. She walked slowly in a circle around Basil and me, taking us in. I can only imagine what the ocelot was thinking, seeing me and a giant Arctic wolf in her territory. I read that ocelots' pee has a lot of oil in it so when they mark their territory, the scent won't wash away as quickly when it rains. Ocelots are fiercely territorial animals—and the bat had obviously brought us directly into her domain.

"Basil, it's a queen ocelot. . . . What do we do?" I whispered. Basil bowed deeply to the ocelot. "Not that kind of queen!" I hissed. Basil stiffened, unsure what her move should be. I was nervous. Only a few seconds passed, but it felt like hours. I tried to remember what else I'd read about ocelots. I'd gone over the entry on them the previous night right before Patter the frog came into our tent. Ocelots are carnivores. Their razor-sharp teeth aren't meant for chewing but rather for tearing flesh from bone. I looked at the regal ocelot. A single ocelot couldn't kill a human . . . right?

Suddenly, the ocelot stepped toward me. Instinctively, I crouched low and kept my eyes trained at the ground. Out of the corner of my eye I could see her slowly stalking toward me. I moved at a snail's pace to lift the flap from my satchel. I reached in and found the last of the dried fish that Noah packed us. I clasped the fish in my hand and pulled it out of my bag. I extended my arm, still not meeting the ocelot's

gaze, and offered it to her. She moved closer . . .
and closer . . . and then, finally, she took the
dried fish from my hand!

The ocelot quickly ate the fish and then sat
down a few feet away from me, calmly licking her

paws clean. I wondered out loud to Basil, "Why isn't she hiding from us? What's going to happen when she finds out I don't have more fish?" Basil uttered a disappointed whimper. "Sorry, Basil. I had to use the fish. I don't know why there's not more. . . . Take it up with Noah when we get home."

?

Wolves don't need to eat every day . . . you'll be fine, Basil.

The ocelot stood up and walked so close to me I could have reached out and touched her. I noticed the beautiful spots on her body, called **rosettes**. The ocelot rubbed herself against my legs and began purring. "I'm going to call you Rosie," I said softly to her. She purred even louder.

Suddenly, she took a few steps away from me and then quickly ran back, weaving herself between my legs where I was standing and then running a few steps forward again. She wanted me to follow her!

I started walking behind Rosie. She led me alongside the tower and then down a steep hill where the ruins seemed to disappear. Basil followed behind me. But then Rosie stopped walking and sat down. I looked at her, and then at Basil. And then I noticed that some dirt on the ground had been dug away, revealing stone. Bedrock? No. This stone was the same as the stone from the ruins. I crouched down and ran my hand across it. This stone was *part* of the ruins. They continued underground! There must be a series of tunnels that connected this section of the ruins all the way back to the tower!

And that's when I heard it. At first, I thought it was another ocelot somewhere in the jungle, or maybe even a parrot in the trees. I listened and heard it again. A faint meow was coming from the ground where Rosie was sitting. Rosie meowed loudly back. I lowered myself to the ground and pressed my ear directly against the cold gray slab. I heard the little meow again.

It was at this moment that I knew. We found
the **baby ocelot!**

I'm sure its mother had been searching
everywhere for it until she discovered it was
trapped in an underground chamber of the
ruins. Who knows how many days it'd been
there?

Rosie pawed at the ground. Her claws were
sharp, but not sharp enough to dig through

stone. Why wouldn't she go into the ruins to rescue her baby?

I walked with Rosie back to the entrance. As I got close to the opening, she retreated to the bushes. She was scared of the tower! But why? I realized there was only one way to find out. I grabbed the lantern from my bag and Basil touched her nose to it, lighting it. I took a step toward the shadowy entrance. I looked back and gave a confident nod to the kitten's mom, hoping she would understand my resolve to help her, and then Basil and I stepped into the tower.

CRUNCH.

CRUNCH.

My boots shifted on the unstable ground. We were walking on something that made noise with every step we took. I looked down and

gasped in horror. It seemed impossible, but holding my lantern to the ground confirmed my fear. We were walking on bones. Everywhere I looked there were skulls of small dead animals, tiny bones, and vertebrae. Basil stood next to me. Her slender body curled protectively around me as we took in the grisly scene. I noticed something else peculiar too. . . .

Feathers! It was a NEST! Suddenly there was movement in the corner of the chamber. Sunlight shone down through cracks in the tower walls. From behind a stone pillar, a massive gray bird stepped into the light . . . a harpy eagle.

The harpy eagle had a dark body with a white belly, striped tail feathers, and a gray head. Its distinguishing feature—the feathers that stuck out above its head—resembled a crown. I recognized it instantly from the book of birds I studied up in the jungle trees. Harpy eagles are large enough to capture, kill, and eat small mammals like monkeys and sloths. Those were the animals whose bones I had just been walking on. I eyed the eagle's enormous talons, the sharp claws that had carried all of these animals here to this tower, as they clacked on the stone floor of the ruins.

Harpy eagles are one of the biggest members of the eagle species. And they have the largest talons of any eagle! They live in the deepest regions of the jungle. They actually prefer to stay beneath the forest canopy, often making their nests in sturdy trees with big, forked branches that can support their considerable weight. I looked above me and noticed a large branch running through the tower. Of course. This was the *perfect protected place for a* harpy eagle nest.

This is why Rosie didn't dare enter the tower. She was afraid of this eagle. An adult ocelot could kill a young harpy eagle, but this one was full grown. And an adult harpy eagle would certainly be capable of killing a small ocelot. That's when it hit me . . . Rosie's kitten!

My theory is that the baby ocelot was hunted by this harpy eagle, who caught it and brought it back to its nest. But the scrappy little ocelot somehow got away and hid inside the ruins. And now, it was trapped. The tower must be the only way in and out of the ruins, and the injured ocelot certainly wouldn't risk trying to escape back through the tower where the harpy eagle nested. But being stranded without food and water, the baby ocelot wouldn't be able to last more than a couple of days.

The eagle took another step toward us. I looked around the tower frantically, trying to formulate a plan. I saw a small crawl space to my right, opposite the entrance. The harpy eagle stood directly in front of us. Suddenly, something small and white moved in the corner behind us. **An eaglet!** The tiny fuzzball hopped forward, looking at us curiously. That was when I realized how dangerous our situation really was. With me and Basil standing between the harpy eagle and her young, the mama eagle was going to defend her nest with all her strength. If we didn't leave the nest right now, she would have every right to attack us. I looked at the eagle's sharp curved beak and talons. She could injure me and Basil pretty badly. I imagined going to school with several new scars on my face from the harpy eagle. What would Mathilda think of me then?

It's a harpy eagle thing, Mathilda . . .

you wouldn't understand.

I couldn't believe I was worrying about Mathilda at a time like this. Suddenly, the eagle stepped forward, unfurling her impressive six-foot wingspan. Basil and I spun to the side, our backs now to the open entrance of the tower. The eagle stepped toward her baby. I had to make a split-second decision to avoid an attack: should Basil and I run deeper into the ruins, through the crawl space, or should we turn and run out of the tower, hoping we could find another way in to save the ocelot kitten?

For me, there was only one option.

"On three," I whispered to Basil, pointing to the tunnel. "One . . . two . . . THREE!" I turned off my lantern, plunging the tower back into darkness. We sprinted in the direction of the crawl space, past the eagle and eaglet, and dove into the small opening. We crawled as fast as we could through cobwebs and vines.

We continued like this for several hundred feet until I felt safe enough to stop to catch my breath. Basil and I looked behind us to see if the eagle had pursued us down the tunnel. I heaved a sigh of relief when I realized we were alone.

Basil relit my lantern and we continued crawling through the tunnel until it opened up into a small room with stairs leading underground. At this point, I was thinking this rescue might be a piece of cake. I wasn't going to fail the mission after all! We'd gotten past the harpy eagle. Now we just needed to find the kitten and get out of the ruins. Well, it turns out I was wrong—very, very, VERY wrong.

Basil and I walked down the stairs and into a long hallway. I noticed the floor of the ruins changed from rectangular stone tiles to square stone tiles.

One stone slab looked different from the others. It wasn't cracked at all and was a bit raised. I thought, could it be a pressure plate? If it was and we stepped on it, it could activate some type of trap. I wondered if the baby ocelot had set it off. I looked around for signs that the trap had been deployed but did not see any. Perhaps the ocelot didn't weigh enough to activate it.

I started to brainstorm ideas for how we could continue down the hallway without stepping on it. Maybe we could jump over it? Unlikely we'd be successful, as the ceiling was quite low. I thought about putting my hands on the wall and my feet on the opposite wall and trying to move sideways in a plank position, but one mistake and I'd fall directly onto the pressure plate. All of a sudden, Basil took off down the hallway at full speed. She stepped directly on the pressure plate. Whizzing noises began echoing down the hall. Arrows were shooting out of the walls!

The arrows were fast. But Basil was faster.
She ran down the hallway and looked back at me
as the arrows hit the opposite wall and fell to
the ground.

"You're lucky that worked," I said. Basil

beamed, a smug look on her face. "Really lucky," I added.

Now it was my turn. I approached the pressure plate. There was no way I'd be able to run as fast as Basil, but maybe I didn't have to. I took my right foot and held it out in front of me and stepped firmly on the plate, pressing it down. Then I quickly took a few steps backward. I could hear the sound of pistons releasing, but no arrows shot out. Just as I suspected, all the arrows had been used on Basil's sprint down the hall. I cautiously walked to where Basil was waiting for me. My lantern was still shining brightly, so Basil and I continued deeper into the ruins. I called out to the baby ocelot, "Hello? We're here to help you!" but I didn't hear any response.

The next room we entered had stairs down to a pit and then stairs on the opposite side where we could see an open passageway. Suddenly, Basil fell forward and tumbled down the stairs. It was strange to see the most graceful and sure-on-her-feet member of my pack make such a clumsy move. The next thing I knew, I was falling down the stairs as well. I landed on my stomach.

My lantern fell out of my hand and rolled several feet in front of me, but it stayed lit. I stood, walked over and picked it up, and returned to the spot at the top of the stairs where both Basil and I had fallen. I leaned down and examined the thin wire that stretched from one side of the hall to the other, with no way to go around. A tiny ocelot would have simply run underneath it, but Basil and I got caught.

"Trip wire," I said. "I wonder how this got here. . . ."

I was interrupted by a strange noise. I didn't want to hear it at first. But it was unmistakable. The sound of pistons moving inside the walls. We'd set something in motion. Most likely something terrible. We just didn't know what yet. I ran down the stairs to Basil, and we stood in the middle of the room, awaiting our fate from the trip-wire trap.

It started with just a few drops of water down the sides of the walls of the ruins. Then drops turned into a steady trickle. I held my lantern to the wall and the mossy stone bricks glistened. Water was seeping into the chamber from all around us. Before I knew it, an inch of water had collected on the floor. Suddenly, the staircase retracted into the walls and one of the stone bricks above us moved and water started pouring into the chamber. Now there was a foot of water on the floor! I looked around the room for another exit, but everything had been sealed off by the pistons. We were trapped!

Basil and I stood huddled together in the middle of the room as the water reached my knees. Now would be a good time for a brilliant idea. The trouble was, I didn't have one. The room couldn't possibly fill *all* the way up with water, could it? But the water showed no signs of stopping. In fact, it seemed like it was rushing out of the opening with more force than ever. It was above my waist now, and Basil had started treading water.

"Basil, you're pushing on my leg." I glanced over at Basil, only to discover she was now on the opposite side of the room from me. "Wait, if that's not you that's touching my leg, then who . . ."

The water swirled in front of me, and then out of the current came the smooth, spotted body of a twenty-foot green anaconda.

I couldn't believe what I was looking at, but

one thing was certain: Basil and I had about ten seconds to figure a way out of this room or we were going to end up as snake food. The green anaconda is an amazing swimmer. Like . . . a much-better-than-Noah amazing swimmer. In fact, swimming is the anaconda's preferred method of transportation. They're part of the family Boidae, or Boa for short. Unlike snakes that kill their prey using venom, an anaconda will wrap its massive body around its meal and constrict it. It squeezes so tightly that it prevents the heart of the animal (or human, *gulp*) from pumping blood to the brain. Once the snake's target is dead, its neck stretches to devour its prey. It can swallow animals as large as a deer. And the tops of their mouths are equipped with backward-pointing teeth that push their food down into their stomach. Very cool. But . . . less cool if you're trapped in a room with one.

I scanned the water and noticed a glowing light in one of the corners of the room. Maybe there was somewhere for the water to drain out behind the wall? I took a huge breath and dove down into the murky water. I swam up to the glowing stone brick and noticed that moss was growing into the cracks around it in a different way than the rest of the stones.

I pushed it into the wall. It moved! Water

started flowing through the square opening. I looked down into it. It was the opening to an **aqueduct**—a series of water troughs built on an incline to move water from one place to another!

I was excited to swim up and tell Basil we were saved. But when I turned around, I was suddenly more afraid than ever. I was face-to-face with the anaconda. Its dark eyes were staring directly into mine.

I wanted to scream, but I was underwater.

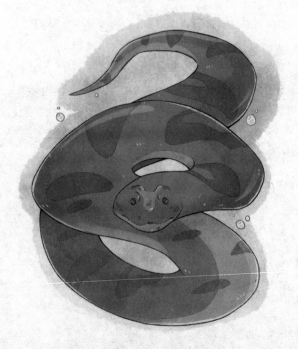

I had to clasp my hand to my mouth to keep air bubbles from escaping. Out of nowhere, Basil swooped down and tugged me away from the anaconda. The snake glided past me, squeezing through the hole and disappearing down the aqueduct. I swam up to the surface and took a deep breath. That was a close one!

After all the water drained, Basil shook herself dry and I wrung out my hair and my clothes. I inspected the inside of my bag to make sure my journal wasn't soaked. Luckily, the plastic bag I kept it in had remained sealed.

There's no telling how long that anaconda had been trapped

in the walls of the ruins. Anacondas only need to eat every four to six weeks, so it could have been a very long time. If it'd really been here that long, we're extremely lucky we didn't become its meal. It's free now (thanks to us) to find its way back to whatever lake or river the aqueduct is connected to. I'm happy for it; however, we're still trapped in this room. What if we never figure out a way to escape? Will Everest and the rest of my wolves start to worry and come find us? Will we survive until then? Basil is doing her best to comfort me, but I'm really beginning to think we might never get out of here. . . .

4:35 p.m.

Good news . . . we're alive! This would be a pretty sad journal if that wasn't the case. Yep, we finally made it out of the chamber—and I have Basil to thank for it. She traced our steps back to the trip-wire trap and followed the trip wire over to the wall that it fed into. I went over to her and inspected what she'd found. I reached my hand into a crevice in the wall and, sure enough, there was a lever!

Once I toggled the lever back up, the pistons

behind the
walls moved
again and
the doors
reappeared.
We continued
deeper into
the ruins
when all of a
sudden . . .

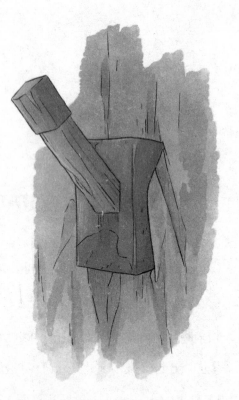

"Meow."

I heard
the kitten! It was close by!! It had to be
somewhere in the room we'd just entered. I
reached into my bag and pulled out my lantern.
Basil pressed her nose to the lantern, lighting
it and immediately filling the room with a warm

glow. I looked around frantically. There in the corner, the baby ocelot lay trembling.

I ran to it and grabbed my sweater from my bag to wrap around the tiny cat. The ocelot kitten was smaller than I had expected— and I had expected a very tiny ocelot. He was

M-I-N-I-S-C-U-L-E (as you might have guessed, that word means super tiny). From my bag, I took my canteen and a small dropper my wolf Tucker had slipped in while we were packing. I placed a few beads of water on the ocelot's

tongue. The ocelot lapped them up, and so I gave him a couple more drops. I couldn't help but smile, realizing that he would make it. We'd gotten to him just in time.

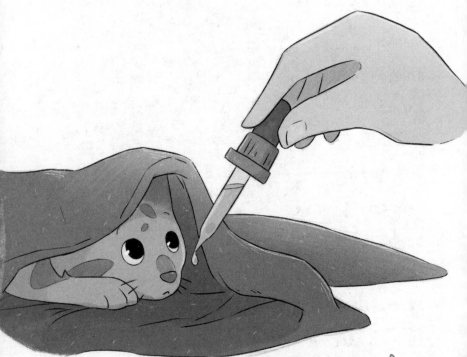

Note to self: thank Tucker for packing a dropper.

The ocelot sucked on the empty dropper and then let out a small whimper. "Aww, you want some more?" I was instantly reminded of a book I'd checked out from the library, Oliver Twist, where the main character, an orphan, asks for more food. The ocelot wriggled in my arms. I told him, "I'm going to call you Twist!"

I plunged the dropper back into my canteen and sucked up the last of my water. Twist happily lapped it up, but I could hear his tiny belly rumbling. He needed food, and we didn't have any to offer him. I knew right then that I was wrong to think we'd finished this rescue. We were still in danger of losing him unless we could reunite him with his mother. She would know exactly how best to care for him. We needed to get out of the ruins quick.

But how? There was no way we could leave the same way we'd come in. We could get stuck in another trap again. And I hadn't forgotten about the harpy eagle. What would she do if we brought the baby ocelot back to her nest? Besides, even if we could make it past all those obstacles again, it would take too much time. Twist needed food fast. And there wasn't anything to eat in the ruins. There had to be another way out.

I looked around. I didn't see any other way except the way we'd come in. And then a brilliant idea came to me (if I do say so myself). We didn't need to look around . . . we needed to look UP! Rosie had already exposed the roof of the ruins aboveground. She was probably above us at this very moment. I could use my pickaxe to break

through the ceiling to the jungle from right
here!

Basil, understanding what I was about to
do, curled up on the ground as far away from
where I would be breaking rock as she could. I
carefully nestled Twist in Basil's warm fur.

As quickly
as I could, I
gathered the
largest and
flattest rocks
from around
the ruins and
stacked them
on top of each
other to create
a makeshift staircase up to the ceiling. I held

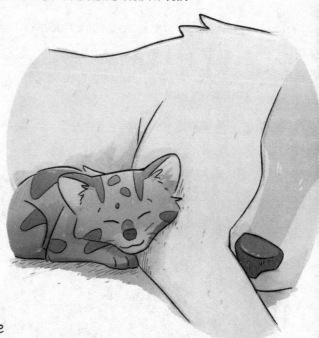

my pickaxe with both my hands and drove it into the stone above. To my surprise, it began to crumble and fall in front of me! I continued for several minutes until finally, after one particularly hard hit, sunlight streamed down into the ruins. I kept swinging the pickaxe up against the hole until enough stone broke away that I could see the trees, bushes, and . . . Rosie, the ocelot!

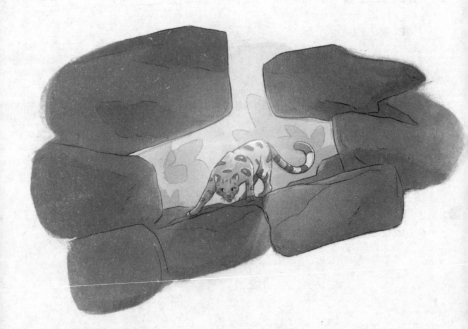

I scrambled down the rock pile to where Basil was and scooped Twist up to show him to Rosie. I balanced on one leg and stretched up as far as I could toward the opening, lifting Twist above my head.

Rosie crouched down and grabbed Twist
by the scruff of his neck. She pulled him up. He
was out of the ruins! But I lost my balance and
toppled down. Luckily, Basil was there to catch
me. We hugged, celebrating the fact that the
rescue was finally finished. I was so excited to
see Rosie and Twist together. I climbed back
up the rocks and eyed the opening. I decided I
was going to go for it. I jumped up as high as
I could, my fingers digging into the cool dirt
around the opening in the stone.

I pulled myself up, wriggling my body through the opening and then swinging a leg up and pushing the rest of the way out of the hole. Rosie was there with Twist. He was nibbling on some fish that Rosie must have caught while we were gone.

Suddenly, I noticed that Basil had not followed me out of the ruins. I ran back over to the opening and looked down. I saw Basil looking at my stone staircase with an uneasy expression. Of course. It couldn't hold her weight. Even if she managed to ascend the wobbly stairs, she wouldn't be able to pull herself up the way I had. I couldn't believe I just left Basil down there alone! I was so excited to see Twist reunited with his mother that I wasn't thinking clearly. I lowered myself back down into the ruins where Basil was standing.

"We'll find another way out," I said to Basil, cupping her head in my hands. She shook her head back and forth. No.

"I'm not leaving you here!" I cried. Basil pointed back into the ruins the way we'd come. It was clear what she wanted to do. She wanted to run back the way she came in. I thought about it. Maybe without me there to slow her down, she would be able to do it. But it was risky. I allowed myself to think of all the terrible things that could happen to her. I imagined waiting on the surface with Rosie and Twist; I imagined the sick feeling in my stomach I would get if Basil was taking too long. I pictured her in the clutches of a huge anaconda.

As much as I didn't want to, I decided to

trust Basil's instincts and let her go. It was the only way. "Please be safe, Basil," I said, hugging her as tears ran down my cheeks. "Run as fast as you can, okay? I love you."

Before I could say another word, Basil disappeared back into the ruins. Once again, I steadied myself on the rock stairs, eyed the ledge above me, and jumped out to grab it. My arms were weaker doing this for the second time. But I was determined to get to the surface, and maybe even run back to the tower in case Basil needed my help getting past the harpy eagle. I grunted and strained to pull myself up, when all of a sudden, I felt a tug on my shirt collar. I assumed it was Rosie trying to help lift me up through the hole. She was much stronger than I realized. I wriggled my way onto the jungle floor and stood up, brushing the dirt and dust off me. But when I turned around, I was surprised to see a pair of familiar yellow eyes—Basil.

I couldn't believe it. Basil had run through the ruins so quickly that she had been the one who had lifted me up out of the hole. She really is the fastest wolf in the entire world. I hugged her again. Rescue mission accomplished!

Basil ran off to fill the canteen and find us something to eat. Meanwhile, Rosie was busy tending to Twist, who was already starting to show more of his happy-go-lucky personality now that he was safe and back with his mother. Before I knew it, Basil returned with some delicious fruit for me to eat. Ever since then, I've been sitting here munching away, updating this journal. I don't want to forget any part of the epic adventure we had in the ruins.

5:43 p.m.

I am sooooooo tired. Basil and I have been sitting around the fire for over an hour with Rosie and Twist. I've been holding Twist, petting him while he naps. Rosie has wandered off a few times to hunt birds and lizards for when Twist wakes up. All I want to do right now is curl up with him in my arms and drift off to sleep in front of the fire. I'm pretty sure I could sleep for fifteen hours!

6:37 p.m.

Whoops! I nodded off a couple times, but Basil woke me with a gentle nudge. I looked at my watch and I realized Basil was right, it was time to leave. After all, I have school in the morning!

I ruffled the spiky fur on top of Twist's head and gave Rosie a scratch under her chin. It was my way of saying goodbye to them. Of course, I didn't want to say goodbye at all. I wished more than anything they could come home with us, but I knew they couldn't. I really hope we can come back here someday—maybe even see Twist again when he's grown up!

What I imagine Twist will look like as an adult ocelot!

Suddenly, Rosie grabbed Twist by the scruff of his neck and ran into the bushes. It was an abrupt goodbye, but I tried not to let it hurt my feelings. We needed to get on our way too. But then something at the edge of the forest made me realize why Rosie ran off so fast. . . . Through the bushes, I could see the jaguar's fierce golden eyes staring back at me.

Before I knew what was happening, Basil
had me on her back and was sprinting through
the jungle. I clung
tightly to her fur
as I looked back
to see the jaguar
in close pursuit.
Its coat was a vivid
orange and yellow with
giant black rosettes like
Rosie's. Its markings allowed
the jaguar to blend into the
jungle forests just like ocelots do.

Jaguars are the third-largest cat species
in the entire world, behind tigers and lions. The
jaguar is at the very top of the food chain here,
which was why it was so concerning that the

big cat was currently gaining on us. I have to admit I was really happy to see a jaguar while we were here in the jungle . . . I just would have preferred to see one from a little bit farther away. If the jaguar succeeded in hunting us, at least it would be quick—jaguars bite through the skulls of their prey, killing them instantly.

"Basil, you're going to have to go faster!" I shouted.

Jaguars can reach speeds of up to fifty

miles per hour. Basil can run faster than

that . . . I hoped. All of a sudden, the jaguar

caught up to us and moved to the side of Basil.

And then it

dawned on me.

We're not being

chased . . .

We're racing!

The jaguar

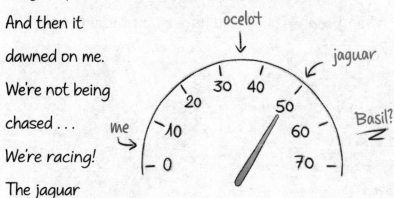

just wants to race! In hindsight, it made

perfect sense. Jaguar attacks on people are

rare. And there would be no way a jaguar had

ever encountered an Arctic wolf before. I

highly doubt it would want to learn if it could

overpower a wolf physically unless it felt

threatened. But a race? Of course. What jaguar

wouldn't want to test their speed against a

worthy competitor like Basil!

Basil and the jaguar raced for several miles before the jaguar finally gave up. Basil must have been taking it easy on our new friend, because she could have beaten it effortlessly

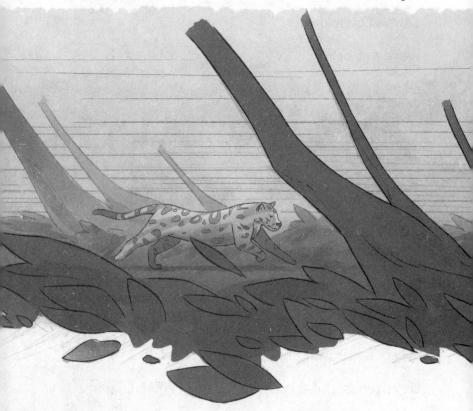

with her super speed. While I was waving goodbye to the jaguar, I realized I was also waving bye to the jungle, Pantanal, the rain forest, and all the amazing creatures we'd encountered on our rescue mission. I'm going to miss this place so much.

Basil spotted a stream, so she stopped to take a long drink for the journey, giving me time to write this entry.
Also, using my compass,

I was able to figure out a faster route home, avoiding the wetlands. It's hard to believe that the next time I write in this journal, I'll be back in the taiga. I really didn't expect to fall in love with the jungle and its animals the way that I did. I'm heartbroken to leave, but I know I will carry the magic of this biome with me for the rest of my life.

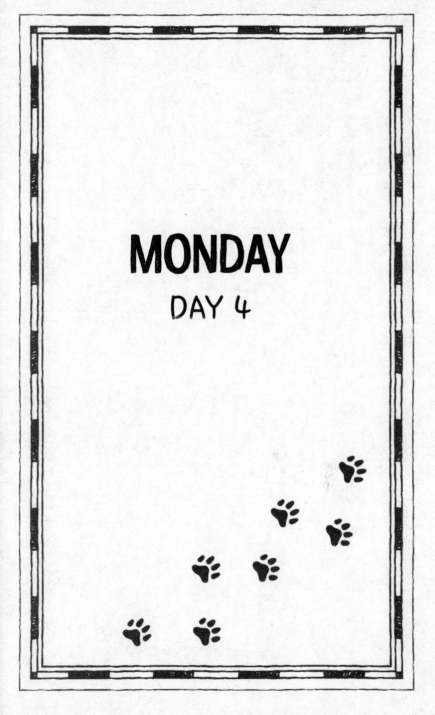

MONDAY

DAY 4

4:57 a.m.

I didn't sleep well riding on Basil's back. Most
of the time she was running so fast that I had
to stay awake just to hang on! But I did sleep
some, and it was a wonderful moment when
I woke up to the familiar smells of our taiga
forest. *Home!* I hopped off Basil and stumbled
into the cave, suddenly realizing how exhausted
I was. Everyone was so happy to see me. Wink
tackled me to the ground and licked my face.
The other wolves, Addison, Everest, Tucker, and
Noah all greeted me and helped me to a seat in

the rocking chair next to a roaring fire. Basil staggered groggily to the back of the cave. I blinked, and the next thing I knew, she was curled up, fast asleep.

Page and Molly nestled at my feet. And Milquetoast and Pipsqueak fought over who got to sit on my lap. Finally, they found a way to both sit on me. Addison brought me a warm bowl of mushroom stew that I quickly slurped down,

and then I told the story to the wolves, who were all eager to hear of our adventure in the jungle.

I told them first about the axolotl and how we

needed to do everything we could to make sure they don't go extinct. I gave Addison the cacao pod I brought her, and I could almost see the gears turning in her head as she figured out what delicious chocolate recipes she was going to bake (chocolate is toxic to cats and dogs so those treats will be just for me). Noah listened intently when I got to the part about the giant river otters. I could tell he was skeptical at first because he kept shaking his head. It was like he couldn't believe that there were otters in the world twice the size of the otters he swims alongside in the rivers here in our forest.

I started falling asleep telling them about Rosie and Twist. Probably for the best, because I know Everest is not going to like finding out how treacherous our journey became. . . . I'll save those stories for tomorrow. For now, I

am going to bed, cuddling my own tiny ocelot,
Milquetoast.

10:45 a.m.

It's recess right now. Yes, I made it to school! I am still so jet-lagged . . . or rather, Basil-lagged. I wouldn't be here at all if it wasn't for Tucker. He woke me up from a very deep sleep and basically carried me over to where Addison was making breakfast. I kept one eye closed while eating my porridge, this time topped with pieces of the dragon fruit I brought home from the jungle.

During breakfast, I learned what the wolves got up to while I was away. Tucker constructed

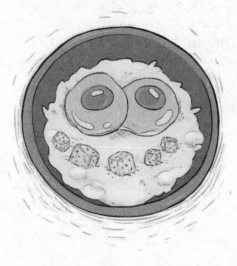

a medicine
cabinet for
the cave and
stocked it with
things like cloth
bandages and
natural salves.
I used some
on my injured
arm and it feels better already! Noah caught
a bunch more fish for everyone to eat, and
Addison baked a salmon pie for Basil to welcome
her home. Wink used his indestructibility to
bulldoze a new room in the back of the cave
(with Everest's supervision, of course). I guess
I really could have that walk-in closet after all,
but I think I'll turn it into a cozy reading nook
instead. It was raining this morning, so I played

a little with Page and Molly inside the cave before putting on my outfit for the day and heading to school. Basil was still asleep when I left. Poor thing, she must be exhausted!

Everest walked to school with me, and I told him about the harpy eagle and the anaconda and the jaguar ... his eyes were so wide with worry that I might have to choose him for the next rescue mission. You'd think he'd trust me more since Basil and I both made it back in one piece!

I said goodbye to Everest at the edge of the forest and walked the rest of the way to school myself. When I got to class, I began to panic when I realized I forgot to do my homework assignment! I was supposed to choose a part of the world to study for a report due next week. And then I remembered ... my library books! I didn't have to lie to the librarian, I *did* have a report due. I was just in such a hurry to get to the jungle it completely slipped my mind. I stuck my hand deep in my satchel and felt around. Luckily, the books were still in my bag. I walked to my teacher's desk and asked if I could do my report on the jungle. My teacher said yes! With everything I saw and learned during the rescue mission, I'd better get an A+. If I don't, I'll have Addison (and Basil) to answer to.

Oh! I just realized I haven't written at all about what I'm wearing today. My outfit is inspired by my trip to the jungle. I have a piece of green ribbon in my hair for the parrot, bright blue rain boots that remind me of Patter the frog, a yellow-and-white polka-dotted shirt in honor of Rosie and Twist, and . . . my overalls that still have quite a bit of mud on them. Of course, as soon as recess began, Mathilda Lemming had something to say about my outfit. But I just shrugged and walked past her.

What does it matter what she thinks? I am an animal rescuer!